GOR /CH

We hope you enjoy this book.
Please return or renew it by the due date.
You can renew it at **www.norfolk.gov.uk/libraries**
or by using our free library app. Otherwise you can
phone **0344 800 8020** - please have your library
card and pin ready.
You can sign up for email reminders too.

NORFOLK COUNTY COUNCIL
LIBRARY AND INFORMATION SERVICE

NORFOLK ITEM

Also by Pippa Goodhart

A Dog Called Flow

Ginny's Egg

Pippa
Goodhart

Illustrated by Adria Meserve

troika

Published by TROIKA

First published 2017

Troika Books Ltd

Well House, Green Lane, Ardleigh CO7 7PD, UK

www.troikabooks.com

A CIP catalogue record for this book is available

from the British Library

ISBN 978-1-909991-37-8

1 2 3 4 5 6 7 8 9 10

Printed in Poland

For Nancy,
a special friend

1

An Odd Sort of Egg

Ginny picked up the egg. Its gold-speckled shell shimmered very slightly in the dim light that struggled through the dusty windows of the henhouse. It was the size and shape of a pear, but more like an oversized teardrop, warm and fragile. In some strange way, it seemed strong too.

As Ginny held the egg in her hand, she could feel it throbbing slightly. She took her thumbs away from the shell for a moment to test whether the throbbing came from her own thumb pulses beating on to the egg, but it didn't. The pulsing came from inside the egg. Ginny's tummy beat too, and a cold tingle of excitement suddenly swept through her as she recognised what it was that she was feeling.

'You're alive, aren't you?' she said to the egg. 'There's a chick inside you.' Then she looked at the egg again. 'But it can't be a hen's chick. You're the wrong sort of egg.'

She held the egg's warmth to her cheek. 'You're the wrong colour and you're too big,' she told it. But what other sort of bird could have got into the henhouse and laid the egg? Ginny looked out the window at the high fox-proof fence of the hen run. Something could have flown down into the run from above, but it still didn't make much sense that whatever it was would lay its egg, and then just leave it, did it? There were only Gran's six hens in the run now.

'You *must* be a hen's egg – an odd sort of hen's egg,' Ginny said. Ginny often told herself sensible things, but she hardly ever really believed them.

And today, however much part of her wanted the excitement of a mystery egg, what she needed most was ordinary sense. The baby was about to be born, and she didn't want any distraction from that.

'Think sense, Ginny Abbot. Gran's hens lay one egg each every morning.' She looked in the egg basket and counted. 'See! Five eggs, and the one in your hand makes six, and there are six hens. It's a hen's egg. Put it into the basket with the rest.'

But she couldn't ignore the feeling that this egg was different. Cradling the special egg between her hands, she crouched to look around the straw bales that the hens nested on. It didn't take long before she spotted the missing hen's egg. 'There!' she said, and she wasn't sure whether she was pleased or cross to have found it.

Standing up with the two eggs in either hand, she compared them. The egg in her left hand had a dull, ordinary shell, but the one in her right hand shimmered.

The ordinary eggs in the basket were for cooking with, but the thought of breaking the special egg into a bowl and beating it made Ginny feel quite ill. She lifted it up to tilt its glinting shell in the light from the window.

'You're going to hatch out and I've got to look after you, haven't I?' There was no choice. Gran would think it was an ordinary chicken's egg, and cook with it. 'I'll have to keep you secret,' she said.

Ginny opened the soft pouch pocket on the front of her brown jacket and gently tipped the egg into it. Then she cradled it from the outside, guarding and nursing the egg with one hand. With her other hand Ginny scooped grain into the chickens' food trough and filled their water bowl. She had to let go of the precious pocket as she picked up the egg basket and opened the shed door. Quickly shooing the hens back in, she refastened the door and was glad to cradle the pocket again. Somehow, even though the pocket was deep and soft, the egg didn't feel properly safe unless she was holding it.

Ginny walked
back up the garden
to Gran's house.
There had been a
gale blowing last
night. Small puffs of cloud still moved fast, high
up in a blue sky. The garden bore scars from the
wind. Twigs and loose flowerpots scattered the
lawn. It was as though some giant had taken a
huge spoon and stirred it all around the garden,
thought Ginny. She remembered lying awake
and hearing the growing drumbeat of wind
banging around the house, pulling at a loose,
clattery gutter and scratching twigs like witches'
fingers on the
windowpanes.

'I wonder if your mother laid you during that storm?' Ginny whispered to whatever is was that was alive in her pocket. 'Could you hear the wind from inside your shell? Were you frightened?'

She looked around her at the windswept, winter garden of greens and browns. A lot of Gran's plants were dead, but tiny, bright white snowdrops and golden-yellow crocus heads waited patiently for the sun to fall on them before they would open out and show their full beauty. Like eggs waiting to hatch, thought Ginny, and she frowned, feeling again the egg's weight in her pocket.

Gran stood waiting for Ginny at the back door.

'Are you all right, sweetheart?' she asked. 'You look as broody as one of my old hens! What have you got on your mind? Is it Mum and the baby?'

'Sort of,' said Ginny. The truth was that she hadn't thought about the baby since she had decided to take the egg, but Mum and the baby made a good excuse to talk about something else.

'Yes,' Ginny said. 'Mum's been having backache and pains all morning, and Dad's stayed home from work. They think that the baby might be coming.' Saying that brought all the other excitement fluttering back to her. A baby brother or sister at last!

'I know,' said Gran, and she ruffled Ginny's springy hair. 'Mum telephoned me. I was just coming to tell you that she wants you home now so that they can say goodbye. They'll be off to the hospital very soon.'

Ginny didn't wait. She thrust the basket of eggs into Gran's hands, and was off.

'I'll follow as soon as I've locked up here,' Gran called after her, but Ginny wasn't listening. She was running down the road and, Gran noticed, running in a strangely lopsided way, as her hand clasped something in her pocket.

2

Bottoms

It didn't take Ginny long to run down the road from Gran's house to her own home. When she raced through the back door she found Mum sitting in the kitchen, a bit pale and a bit shiny-eyed and with her hands resting on her bulging tummy.

'You're in a hurry!' she said as Ginny raced in. 'Take your jacket off, love, and have some breakfast with me before we go. They'll starve me at the hospital – I remember that from last time – so Dad is doing me some toast and honey. Would you like some?'

Then something gripped tight inside Mum and she clutched the chair seat and panted. Ginny hadn't realised that it would hurt Mum so much having the baby, but Mum and Dad looked happy so she supposed that everything was all right.

'OK, Maggie?' asked Dad, gently stroking Mum's head. Ginny smiled when she saw that he had cut Mum's toast and honey into soldiers as he had used to do for her when she was little.

'Don't you laugh at your old dad!' he told her. 'We need to look after Mum. She's got a big job ahead of her.'

Mum blew out as if to blow away the pain that had held her a moment before, then she and Dad smiled together.

Ginny began to unbutton her jacket, and then she remembered – the egg.

'Oh!' she said out loud.

'What is it?' asked Dad.

'Oh, nothing. I'll be down again in a minute.' She ran out of the room and up the stairs. It was so annoying! She didn't want to have to bother with the silly egg when Mum was about to have their baby! But she couldn't hang up the jacket downstairs. The egg could easily get squashed and broken.

Up in her room, Ginny pulled her jacket off quite roughly but put her hand into its pocket more gently. As she touched the egg and felt again its hum of hidden life, she knew why she had taken it. It was hers to care for.

Ginny arranged her jacket into a ring shape on her bed. It was still warm from her body and would keep the egg cosy while she said goodbye to Mum and Dad. She gently placed the egg in the centre of the jacket nest.

'See you soon,' she promised as she headed back to the stairs, and then laughed quietly at herself for talking to an egg.

Back in the kitchen, Mum was eating her honey soldiers and trying to organise.

'Remember that tomorrow is dustbin day and . . .'

Dad was writing the hospital's phone number down for Ginny and Gran.

Mum looked at her watch. 'And then we must go, Stephen,' she said.

'Yes, love,' said Dad. 'Everything's ready, and I can see Gran coming down the road.'

Ginny suddenly realised that this was the last time it would be just her and Mum and Dad.

'Can we do Bottoms?' she asked. 'We haven't done that for ages!'

'Yes,' said Mum. 'One last time before we have a tiny new bottom to join the gang.' She heaved herself bulkily out of her chair.

Bottoms was a family chant that had started when Ginny was four and full of questions. She had asked, 'Dad, what is "a bot"?'

Dad had looked puzzled but answered, 'Well, I suppose that "bot" must be short for bottom, and "a bot" must be one bottom. Why?'

And Ginny had said, 'Because that's us.' Dad had still looked blank, so Ginny had explained, 'It's our name, silly! Abbot – a bot.'

And out of that had grown the Bottoms ritual

that Mum and Dad and Ginny did, usually when they were saying goodbye or celebrating coming together again, but never in public. All three of them would stand back to back and bump their bottoms together as they chanted, 'Mummy A-bot, Daddy B-bot, Ginny C-bot. As you can *see*, we are a fami*ly* of one, two, *three* Bottoms!' And then they twizzled round and joined arms in a three-cornered hug.

They did it now, and the hug was stretched almost beyond Ginny's reach by Mum's great tummy full of baby.

'What are you all up to?' laughed Gran as she came in and caught them in the middle of it.

'Oh,' said Mum. 'We were just doing Bot–' but then she sucked in her breath as another pain clenched her. She leant on Dad and puffed and panted her way through it while Dad rubbed her back. Ginny held Mum's hand and, as the pain passed, Mum winked encouragingly at Ginny's worried face.

'Take care of Ginny for me,' she told Gran. 'I promise we'll ring with news as soon as there is any.' She saw Ginny open her mouth to speak and added, 'Yes, Gin, even if it *is* the middle of the night! I'll be wanting to tell you about the baby anyway. I don't think I could bear to wait until a sensible time to telephone!'

'Good,' said Ginny.

Mum and Dad went.

'And you and I are just going to have to wait now, my lovely,' Gran told Ginny. 'It'll probably be several hours before the baby arrives. You can go round to Sophie's to play if you like?'

'Sophie's away for half-term,' said Ginny. 'And, besides, I've got something that I want to do in my bedroom, if that's all right?'

'That's fine,' said Gran. 'I'll do some baking in the kitchen.' Gran did a little dance. 'Oh, I do wonder what this baby will be like!'

'So do I,' said Ginny.

3

Waiting

Ginny spent most of the day in her bedroom just holding and warming the egg. She tried to imagine what its chick would be like.

Suddenly a phone bleeped downstairs and Ginny was jolted out of her dreamy mood. Could it be news of the baby? She pulled up her shirt. Placing the egg against the warmth of her tummy, and tucking the bottom of her shirt back into her waistband, she secured the egg in place. Then, pulling down her baggy jumper to hide the tell-tale bulge, she headed for the stairs.

In the kitchen, Gran had snatched her phone from her pocket without even pausing to wipe pastry mix from her fingers, but Ginny could see from her face that it wasn't giving her news of the baby.

'Insurance? No, no, I don't want any. No. And I'm waiting for an important phone call. Goodbye.'

Gran grinned at Ginny as she looked at the phone in her hand. 'Look what a mess I've made of it!' She wiped the phone with the bottom of her apron. Then she noticed that Ginny was clutching her middle. 'Have you got tummy-ache, love?' she asked.

Ginny shook her head, but Gran looked at the hand on her tummy.

'I'm going to bring you a quilt, and make you snug and warm on the sofa,' she said. 'We don't want you getting ill and not being able to see Mum and the baby.'

Ginny let herself be tucked up under a quilt, and accepted a hot drink. It was nice resting and nursing the egg in warm, hidden peace while her mind wondered about the days ahead. How was she going to care for the chick once the egg had hatched? How long could she keep it a secret?

Gran brought Ginny a jam tart fresh from the oven. 'Careful, mind,' she said. 'The jam'll be a

lot hotter than
the pastry.'
Then she
saw Ginny's
face and added,
'You look as if your
thoughts are miles away!'

'Oh, I was just thinking. You know,' said
Ginny.

'Yes, I know.' Gran smiled.

But this time, thought Ginny, Gran didn't
actually know. She felt a bit guilty, keeping the
egg secret from Gran. It was Gran's egg, after

all, and Gran was an especially nice person, and should be told things.

Ginny's gran was a small, stocky lady, not much taller than Ginny herself, and her grey hair was cut short in a no-nonsense style. Yet Gran was beautiful. Her eyes sparkled, and she moved with the easy grace. Her clothes weren't fussy either. They were practical and tough but she added special scarves or jewellery, which always had a story to them. Today she was wearing the lovely mother-of-pearl brooch that Grandad had given her when Ginny's mum was born.

'Gran?' said Ginny. 'Did you wear that brooch on the day that I was born? Are you wearing it for the baby being born today?'

'Yes,' said Gran, and she sat down on the sofa beside Ginny's covered toes. 'Except that you weren't born in the daytime.'

Ginny had heard this story many times before, and she loved it. 'Go on,' she said.

'Well,' said Gran. 'Maggie, your mum, went into labour in the early hours of midsummer morning, and she and your dad went off to the hospital. Owen, your grandad, and I spent all day with fluttering tummies, waiting and wondering about our first grandchild. Well, we heard nothing all day, and it got later and later. We busied ourselves with all sorts of jobs that didn't take us too far from the telephone. I remember that Owen cleaned out the drain, and I made so much strawberry jam that I ran out of jam jars and ended up storing it in tea cups and bowls and whatever else was to hand because I didn't want to leave the house long enough to see if a neighbour could lend me any jars. We were waiting together for news of the baby.'

'Like us now,' said Ginny.

'That's right,' said Gran. 'Anyway, by midnight we had run out of jobs and we decided that we really should go to bed. I pinned my mother-of-pearl brooch on to my nightie. I don't know why, really. I just felt that it was a link between me and your mum. Margaret means pearl, you know. That's why Owen had chosen a mother-of-pearl brooch for me when Maggie was born. Of course, Owen was soon fast asleep and snoring, but I lay in bed wide awake. I was far too excited to sleep. And then, at last, the phone rang! Well, I jumped to answer it, but I found that I was stuck. The brooch had tangled with

the blanket, and I couldn't get free! You can't
imagine how I felt, stuck in bed with that phone
ringing on the chest of drawers across the room
with the news that I had been longing for, and
your grandad still snoring beside me! My fingers
were too excited to work properly and I couldn't
untangle the brooch, and all the time I was
sure that whoever was phoning would give up. I
shouted at Owen, but he still didn't wake quickly
enough, so I did something awful.'

Ginny grinned.

'I picked up the vase of flowers that was
on my bedside table, and I poured it over your
grandad's head to wake him! He was soaked, and
the bed was soaked, and there were bits of wet
leaf and flower everywhere, but it didn't matter.
It got Owen to the phone, and in moments he
was saying, "It's a girl! A beautiful little girl, and
they're all fine." Oh, it was a special moment,
that!' Gran gave Ginny a big hug. 'A very special
moment.'

'And then you had to tidy up?' said Ginny.
She didn't want the story to end.

'Yes, then your grandad came and untangled
me, and we danced around the room together!

After a while we cleared up the mess of flowers in the bed. It didn't properly dry out for weeks after, but it was worth it.'

'And you ate peanut butter and bananas on toast and drank cocoa,' finished Ginny.

'Yes. Quite delicious. And now,' said Gran, brushing jam-tart crumbs off Ginny's quilt, 'if you're in the mood for family stories perhaps we could do a bit of that patchwork together?'

Mum and Ginny had started to make a piece of patchwork when Mum was first pregnant, and over the months it had grown almost big enough to make a cot quilt for the baby. Ginny enjoyed cutting out the paper hexagons and carefully stitching the fabrics to them. She enjoyed deciding which bits of material looked nice next to each other even more, and hearing from Mum where each bit had come from. Each patch had a story to tell. There were the bold, stripy pieces that came from the deckchair cover that had torn and sent Uncle Thomas sprawling on the lawn last summer. There was a bit of the pretty blue dress that Ginny had had new for her seventh birthday party, and then spoilt that same day with dandelion stains as she collected food for her new rabbit, Bobby. There was a bit of Gran's old apron that had, at last, fallen to bits but had some good parts at the corners. There was a piece of glimmering white silk left over from Mum's wedding dress. There was a tartan patch that was Dad fabric. It came from a blue checked shirt of his that had been in a wash that had gone wrong and turned everything pink.

Ginny looked at the patchwork now. Just a few more patches and it would be ready for the baby's cot.

'We need something for Grandad,' said Ginny. 'There's nothing for him yet.'

'That's true,' said Gran. 'Will you be all right for a moment if I pop home and see if I can find a scrap of something that will remind us of Grandad?'

So Gran went and fetched a piece of soft, brown checked shirt material that was the sort that Grandad had always worn. While Gran was out of the house, Ginny looked to see that her strange shimmering egg was safe. And then she and Gran sewed and talked and waited for the phone to ring until it was nighttime.

Ginny went to bed early, but she didn't sleep.

She made a small, warm cave for her egg to lie
in by propping up her duvet with one arm. The
light on her bedside table dimly lit the dark
space, and Ginny lay beside the egg, watching
and waiting.

4

Hello, Egg!

Hours passed, and Ginny heard Gran go to bed. The light from the landing went out, and soon after that the egg rocked slightly from side to side, and a muffled, scratching sound joined the soft thumps.

Ginny breathed in sharply as a new hair-thin crack appeared and grew across the smooth surface of the egg. It ran zig-zagging around the waist of the egg, breaking the perfect wholeness, but promising that soon Ginny would see her chick. Ginny's breathing quickened with excitement. The crack spread like a fast-drawn black line, and then the egg lay still for a moment or two, as though whatever was inside had exhausted itself with the effort of cracking the shell. Ginny reached out a finger, wanting to stroke the shell, and whispered, 'Come on, little one. You're nearly out.' But as her finger touched it, the shell suddenly jolted apart into two golden, cupped halves. Lying crumpled between the pieces of shell was something tiny and breathing and damp and greeny-grey.

'A frog!' squeaked Ginny, startled to see something that wasn't any kind of bird chick. But even as she said that she knew it was nonsense. Frogs come from tadpoles that come from little jelly eggs. Then *what*? Perhaps some kind of lizard?

Ginny watched, entranced, as the little creature slowly uncurled and revealed itself, pulling free of the sticky egginess that had stuck it down in an oval huddle and dulled the colours of its body. She watched as the head poked upwards. It had large nostrils, and surprising lines of dark lashes on either side, marking where the eyes were. But the eyes themselves stayed closed. As the unseeing head rose on its long neck, the little body lurched back, and short, scaly, wobbly legs propped up its front half. Another lurch and the back legs were up, and a miniature dragon

stood for a moment before crumpling down again
on to the duvet. Two more faltering tries, and
then he stood firm.

'A dragon! Hello, Egg!' whispered Ginny,
and the dragon's head tipped to one side, trying
to work out where the sound of her voice was
coming from.

'I'll clean you up, and then you'll be able to
see better.'

Ginny gently pushed back her duvet, and
stepped out of bed. She tiptoed quietly along
the landing to the bathroom, then carried back
a tooth mug of warm water. She took a box of

paper tissues from on top of her chest of drawers and knelt beside the bed where the little dragon lay.

In the soft light of her bedside lamp, Ginny carefully dampened a corner of tissue and reached across to wipe the eggy stuff that covered the dragon's face. She wiped on down the ridged, scaly back to reveal the glowing, greeny-blue, purple-grey, magical colours that lay beneath the stickiness.

'Oh, Egg, you're beautiful! Now, don't be frightened. I'm going to lift you on to my lap so that I can wipe properly round your eyes.'

Ginny cupped her hand under the warm, damp little body, and lifted. The tiny dragon had a surprisingly solid feel to him, but he was soft too. Ginny could feel the delicate throb of a heartbeat against the palm of her hand. From head to tail the dragon was no longer than the length of the hand he sat on. Ginny gently took the head between two fingertips and dampened a fresh corner of tissue. Then, very carefully, she wiped over the dark lashes, one side and then the other. When the eggy gunge had been cleaned away, the little dragon's eyes eased open. They

opened slowly and jerkily, as if even the dim glow
from the lamp was too bright for eyes that had
never seen any light before. They were big eyes
for that size of head, dark and deep and round.
The eyes blinked, and then they looked at Ginny
in a puzzled, unfocused way.

'Can you see me now?' said Ginny.

Egg blinked a slow blink of both eyes together.
When they opened again they looked properly at
Ginny. She smiled back.

Ginny washed the rest of the wrinkly little

face, then on down the skin of Egg's neck and belly. By the time she had finished the underside of his legs, the skin on the dragon's face had dried to something like smooth leather. The wrinkled, crumpled, too-long-in-the-bath look had gone, and the little dragon appeared more solid. Then his stumpy green legs suddenly folded down on to the duvet, his eyes closed, and the little dragon fell asleep. 'Worn out by hatching, are you?' whispered Ginny, and she stroked the tiny, flat top of his head.

Ginny herself didn't feel at all sleepy. It was past one o'clock in the morning and everything was dark and quiet, but Ginny had never felt more awake. She lay down in bed, and pulled the duvet over herself and the dragon. Now that he was curled up again in sleep, Ginny could cave the whole of him under one cupped hand. What was she going to do with him? For the moment she was content with his just being there. She watched and wondered.

5

The Baby!

It may have been hours or it may have been just minutes that Ginny stayed like that. But the insistent bleep of Gran's phone ringing in the room next door woke her.

'The baby!' said Ginny.

Ginny leapt out of bed, and hurried to the bedroom next door which had the spare bed, but also the baby's cot waiting and empty. Gran, sitting half-in and half-out of the bed, had poked

the button on her phone, and was holding it to one ear, her face pink and eager. Ginny sat beside Gran, watching her face and trying to guess what she was being told. The one-sided conversation from Gran's end puzzled her.

'Stephen? It is Stephen, isn't it? Yes, you sounded a bit strange, that's all. No, never mind that. Tell me! Tell me about the baby, for goodness' sake!'

And then there was a long gap when Gran didn't say anything. Ginny saw Gran's face fade from excited pink to a dull grey. Gran clutched the phone with two hands now, bending away from Ginny.

'What is it, Gran?' whispered Ginny. 'What's happened?'

But Gran just laid a hand on Ginny's shoulder and went on talking to Dad. 'Oh, Stephen! Of course it's a shock, but it'll be all right, I promise you. And Maggie, how's my Maggie?' There was more talk from the other end, then, 'Give yourselves time, love. It's very early days. You can't expect to know how you really feel straight away.' Then, at last, Gran looked at Ginny, and said, 'Now, Stephen, I've got Ginny here, impatient for news.'

'Let me talk to Dad!' implored Ginny, but Gran turned away again, and listened some more before going on, 'Yes – yes – I'll tell her. Not tomorrow. No, OK. No, don't you worry about us. So, we'll see you in an hour or so's time? Yes, of course. No, I quite understand. Lots of love to Maggie and, and to – has he got a name yet?'

Ginny jumped up from the bed. 'He! You said "he"! It's a boy!'

So there *is* a baby, and he is alive! thought Ginny. She felt as though her heart was safe to start beating again now. For an awful, dry-mouthed couple of minutes she had begun to wonder.

Gran tapped her phone, and put it on the bedside table. Then she stood up, and reached out her arms to hug Ginny. 'You've got a baby brother, my love,' she said in a too-jolly voice that frightened Ginny again. 'But he hasn't yet got a name.'

'But Mum, is Mum all right?' asked Ginny.

'Yes, Mum's fine.' But Gran still wasn't properly looking at her. She wouldn't meet

Ginny's eyes with her own.

'Then what's wrong with the baby?
Something's wrong, isn't it? Tell me, Gran!'
Ginny shook Gran's arm as if she thought she
could shake the information out of her.

'Well,' admitted Gran, 'yes, there is a
problem. But Dad wants to tell you about it
himself when he comes home. Don't worry, love.
It isn't so very bad.'

Back in her bedroom, Ginny reached out for
the tiny bundle of sleeping dragon. She held Egg

close to her chest and curled herself around him
in an egg-shaped huddle under her duvet. 'Oh,
Egg,' she said. 'Something's wrong with our baby,
and they won't tell me what it is.'

6

What Do You Want?

Ginny woke from one of those deep dreams that twists to fit the real world. She dreamt that her bed was coming alive and moving under her, but woke to find that what was moving under her hand was the little dragon waking from his own dreams.

Ginny stroked a finger down Egg's rough, warm back. Egg opened his eyes. 'Hello, funny face,' said Ginny.

Egg focused his dark, deep eyes on Ginny's, and blinked a slow, smiling blink of hello back. He stood himself up, a bit unsteadily, and then his tiny jaw dropped open and stretched into a surprisingly pink yawn. Ginny laughed, but stopped laughing as the yawn suddenly turned into a loud squeal.

'Oh, no! Shush, you silly thing!' She put a
finger to her lips in urgent sign language, even
though she knew that the gesture would mean
nothing to the dragon. Egg tipped back his head,
opened his mouth again, and squealed again.
It was a piercing, demanding noise, and Ginny
instinctively clapped her hand tightly over him,
like a lid.

'Gran might hear!' she whispered. 'Shush!'
Under her hand the squeal came again, and
she could feel tiny, tickling, leathery paw pads
scrabbling at her hand in an attempt to escape.
'What do you want?' asked Ginny, and she lifted
her hand off him, and used a finger to tilt his
head so that she could properly see his face. She
didn't expect the little dragon to answer, but he
did. He opened his mouth and squealed again,
even louder than before. She must do something
to stop that noise! Without really thinking about
it, Ginny sat up in bed, then held and rocked Egg.
As she cradled and rocked, Egg sank down on
his side, his eyes drooped and his mouth closed.
Now that he was quiet, Ginny could think, and it
was suddenly obvious to her what Egg had been
squealing about.

'You're hungry, aren't you?' she said. 'You stay here and be quiet, and I'll get dressed and find you some food.' But the moment she put Egg down, his eyes and mouth opened and the squeals started again. Ginny scooped him into her hands, and rocked them hard. She could hear Gran moving about in her bedroom next door.

'I'm trying to do what you want, you silly thing,' she told him. 'I can't keep rocking you and get food at the same time, can I? Which do you want me to do?' She held Egg up to her face, and looked into his eyes. Egg squealed a long, wobbling, ear-hurting squeal, and a moment later there was Gran's voice outside Ginny's door.

'Are you all right in there, Gin?'

'Yes, Gran.' Ginny tried to sound unflustered. 'I, um, just turned my headphones up too loud.' Still rocking Egg in her left hand, she tapped at her iPod.

Egg put his head on one side, shut his mouth and listened as the music started. Its rhythmic beat seemed to have the same effect on him that rocking had. Gradually Ginny slowed her rocking hand, and then stopped it still. Egg whimpered, but he didn't squeal again. Ginny reached for her half-

empty paper tissue box, and gently laid the dragon down on to the soft white tissues inside it. His mouth stayed shut, and he began to snore softly. Ginny grabbed her dressing gown from the back of her door, and pulled it on. 'I'll be back soon,' she whispered, and then headed quickly for the stairs.

What would a baby dragon eat? He must have eaten egg when he was inside the egg. That was what happened, wasn't it? Baby birds inside eggs must eat the yolk and white of the egg, or there wouldn't be room for them to grow. But as Ginny stepped into the kitchen, thoughts about Egg and eggs disappeared.

'Dad!'

7

There's Something Wrong

Gran was by the window, cutting bread for toast.
Dad was sitting at the table, holding a mug of
coffee in his hands. He looked pale and tired.

'Are you OK, Dad?' Ginny asked. She stood
behind Dad's chair, and wrapped her arms
around his neck. She kissed his rough, unshaven
cheek. Dad patted her hands.

'Yes, love. A bit shaken up, but I'm OK.' Then
Dad took a deep breath. 'Ginny,' he said, and he
pulled her round to face him. 'Ginny, love, our
baby has something wrong with him. He has
Down's syndrome. He has a genetic fault, and
he'll – well – he'll always be a bit different. He
has the distinctive look of a baby with Down's
syndrome, and he will always be a bit slow at

learning how to do things. And . . .' Dad pushed a hand through his hair. 'Oh, it's hard to explain!'

'Do you mean that he's got special needs?' asked Ginny.

Dad looked her properly in the face now. 'Yes. That's it,' he said, relieved that he wouldn't have to struggle to explain more. 'How do you know about things like that?'

'Because there are kids with special needs in school,' said Ginny. 'Mark in the infants has Down's syndrome. You know him. He is Ben in my class's brother.'

'Oh!' said Dad, brightening. 'Well, anyway, the doctors say that our little chap seems to be quite a healthy baby. Perhaps he might go to your school too some day?' Dad did a real smile at last, and picked up his mug and sipped the coffee. 'Euch, its gone cold!' he said. 'I think I'd better make a fresh cup!'

'Let me do that,' said Gran, reaching for the kettle, 'and I'll get you something to eat too.'

Ginny poked Dad in the ribs to get his attention. 'What are we going to call the baby?' she asked. 'And when can I see him and Mum?'

Dad sagged into his chair again. 'We haven't

picked a name yet, love. And Mum doesn't feel ready for visitors.'

'I'm not visitors!' said Ginny. 'I'm *me*!'

'Oh, Ginny, of course you're not ordinary visitors, but Mum really can't face seeing anyone just yet.' Dad paused. 'We weren't expecting any problems with the baby you see, Gin.' He looked at her, willing her to understand, but Ginny frowned. Dad tried again. 'All those jokes that we made about the baby being prime minister, well, we didn't really think that he'd ever be that, of course, but, well, we did think he'd grow up to have a job, and perhaps a family, all those ordinary sorts of things. And now some of those things might never happen. It takes some getting used to.'

'But he's still my brother and your baby! And your grandson, Gran! Don't you want to see him?'

Gran nodded. 'Yes, of course I do, love. But if Mum isn't ready to see us just yet, then it won't do us any harm to wait a day or so until she is. She needs time to work out her own feelings about the baby before she can cope with other people.'

It still didn't make any sense to Ginny. Having Mum and the baby shut away was wrong! 'But . . .' she started to protest.

'Just leave it for now, Ginny,' warned Gran. 'We need to persuade your dad to get some sleep before he goes back to the hospital. Mum's having a rest now – they gave her some pills to help her sleep – but poor Dad hasn't slept since the night before last.'

'But what about the baby?' asked Ginny, getting angry now. 'If Mum is asleep and Dad isn't there, then who is looking after him?'

'The nurses are doing that,' said Gran.

'But he's only less than a day old! He should be with one of us! I'd look after him!'

Dad sighed, and got up wearily from the table. 'I'll go to bed,' he said to Gran.

Ginny got up too. She banged her chair into the table. '*I* could be with him, or you could, Gran! You know how to look after babies. We could do it together.'

Gran stroked a soothing hand over Ginny's head. 'Don't keep going on, love. You've just got to accept things as they are.'

But how could she? They had, all of them – Mum, Dad, Gran and her – longed for this baby for years. Now, at last, he was here, and the adults wanted to behave as if he wasn't! Ginny was about to try again to make *them* understand *her* when she suddenly remembered Egg upstairs in the tissue box.

'Um, can I have an egg for breakfast, please, Gran?'

'Good girl,' said Gran, and she reached for an egg from the rack.

'I'll take my milk upstairs and drink it while I get dressed,' said Ginny. Then, as Gran looked a bit doubtful, she added, 'Mum lets me do it.'

'Oh, go on then,' said Gran. 'Everything's so much at sixes and sevens today that I don't suppose it matters. Mind you don't spill it.'

'I won't,' said Ginny, and she hurried back up the stairs with her cup of milk.

In her bedroom where the music was still playing, the little dragon was snuffling and wriggling a little in his tissue-box bed. As Ginny stripped off her pyjamas and pulled on her clothes, Egg's bright, dark eyes opened. He seemed to slow-blink a hello. Ginny put her hand into the box and carefully lifted him out. She cradled his warm body in one hand, and covered him with the other, leaving his head and tail sticking out either end. She spoke soothingly,

and Egg opened his pink mouth to squeak, but
quite gently this time, in an up-and-down kind
of sound. Then he tipped back his head, opened
his mouth wide, and did one of his really loud
squeals. Ginny glanced towards the door.

'Shush! Yes, I do understand that noise, and
I've brought you some milk.' She let him sniff the
cup of milk, and his tiny tongue flickered towards
it. Ginny set him down on her bedside table
beside the cup of milk. Then she sat and watched
him drink.

She thought of Mum sitting in a hospital bed alone. She would be hating that. Mum was what Dad called 'a very impatient patient', and now she was stuck in hospital and unhappy. Perhaps Ginny could send her some of the patchwork quilt to work on? Ginny wished that she could talk to Mum to cheer her up. But Dad had said 'no' to Ginny phoning her. Well, at least she could write to her, couldn't she?

Ginny reached for her pens and paper. Mum had once told her that green was a soothing colour. Ginny took the light and dark green pens, and made a border of green stripes around the paper. Then she looked at the dark blue, the black and the brown, and decided that those colours looked too gloomy. She wanted to cheer Mum up, so she took the orange, red, light blue and pink to do each letter in turn as she wrote,

Dear Mum,
Please let me come and see you. I want to
meet our baby.
Here is some quilt for you to do.
Love from Ginny
PS I think that you should only sew the

bottom half of each patch. If you turn them over after that, the top will be the new bottom bit, and then you can sew that.

The PS was because Ginny remembered visiting a clock shop where Dad had pointed out how every clock and watch had been stopped at ten to two. 'Because it looks like smiles on the clock faces,' he said. 'It makes the shop seem a happy place, and makes you more inclined to buy something from them.'

Ginny thought that if Mum sewed the bottom part of the hexagons then they too would look like a smile and might help make her happier.

Ginny put everything together, and wrote *For Mum* on the bag. She left it outside Mum and Dad's bedroom door where Dad was bound to trip over it when he came out. Then she took a deep breath and returned to her own room.

Egg was rolling on his back on the floor, fighting with Ginny's prickly hairbrush. Ginny smiled, and tickled Egg's tummy with the tip of a finger.

8

So Strange, So New

Egg liked the soft-boiled egg. Ginny had taken
some up to her room and she fed him little
bits of it on the tip of her finger and felt the
tickle of his tongue as he licked it off. He
drank some more milk too, this time from the
egg cup. He drank with his feet braced apart
to hold himself steady. Egg had plumped out
with the food and drink, and he had stopped
squealing. But he looked around as if he had lost
something. What else might he need? Ginny
curved a hand over his back, and hoped that
made him feel safe and warm.

Ginny was so intent on watching and
wondering about Egg that she didn't notice the
window cleaner until it was too late. The window

cleaner suddenly popped his head up on the other side of the glass and began waving his sponge of soapy water over the window. Egg jumped on to the windowsill.

'Oh no!' said Ginny, but it was too late to hide him.

Egg stretched and pounced after the sponge, and the window cleaner's eyes opened wide and his mouth dropped open. He tested Egg, stopping the sponge still and then suddenly wiping across to the other side of the window. Left and right, up and down, Egg followed, his tail thrashing, a grin on his face, and his colours glowing. The window cleaner looked at Ginny.

'How d'you make it do that?' he called at her through the glass. Ginny grabbed her phone and waved it, poking at it, hoping that it looked like a remote control for a toy.

'I'm going to have to hide you better,' she told Egg as the window cleaner went back down his ladder. 'But you want to play, don't you?'

Ginny put Egg on the table in front of her mirror, wondering what he would do when he saw his own reflection. He squealed . . . and, of course, the reflection dragon opened its mouth and seemed to squeal back. Egg squealed again, even louder.

'Shush! Dad's trying to sleep!'

Egg was jumping at the mirror, nosing at the glass, trying to sniff his new friend. With his scales pulsing with excited colour, Egg went up on to his back legs, and scrabbled at the glass, trying to climb into the mirror. There was a

desperate kind of keenness in his eyes, and Ginny
suddenly knew that this wasn't just a game to
him. He was serious.

'Do you think that dragon's your brother?' said
Ginny. Egg went on bumping his little snout on
to the cold, hard glass, until Ginny gently pulled
him away. 'It's only a reflection,' she told him.
'Not real.'

Egg warbled then, his up-and-down
questioning warble, and waited, head on one
side, seemingly expecting Ginny to give him an
answer, but she couldn't.

'I don't understand,' she told him. 'I don't
know what you want.' She stroked soothingly
down his spine, and offered him some more milk
in the egg cup. But she knew that he wanted
something more than that, and she couldn't think
what it might be.

At suppertime that evening, Dad gave Ginny a
note from Mum. All it said was,

My dear Ginny,
Please come and see me tomorrow. Will you,
sweetheart?

I love you,
Mum XXX

'Brilliant!' said Ginny, hugging Dad hard. 'Can we go first thing?'

Dad nodded, and kissed the top of her head.

It worried Ginny, though. What would she do with Egg when it was time for her to go to the hospital?

At three o'clock the next morning, Egg squealed Ginny awake. She stumbled out of bed to feed and shush him, and she noticed something that jolted her wide awake.

'You've grown!' she said. Egg put his head on one side, and whimpered. 'No, you're not in trouble,' said Ginny. 'It's not your fault.' Ginny picked him up and held him to her cheek. Egg snuffled into her ear, nosing through her tangle of hair, and tickling her. She had to hold him in both hands now. 'No wonder you're a hungry dragon,' she said. 'You're twice the size you were yesterday.'

If he could grow that much in one day, then how big would he have grown in a week? How much would he grow before he stopped growing? Ginny lifted Egg up. 'But you're not any heavier.' That was odd. Ginny gently stroked Egg's bright, smooth scales. As her fingers worked down his back she felt small bumps on his shoulders that she hadn't noticed there before. Egg looked up at her, and his colours glowed brightly for a moment in the dark.

'Oh, my goodness, Egg, you're growing wings!' said Ginny. 'You're growing up.'

Egg half closed his eyes, and began to sing. It was the most beautiful sound that Ginny had ever heard. It was like the noise that you make if you run a wet finger around the rim of a wine glass – high and ringing, and it came and went and buffeted around Ginny's head like a breeze. Part of her wanted him to go on and on with the beautiful song, but part of her was alarmed. It was so very strange, so different and new. The song soared and dipped and rose and spun.

'A flying song,' she suddenly realised, thinking of those wing buds. 'You're going to fly, little Egg. Oh, lucky you!'

She knew he could leave her on the ground when he did.

Ginny leant back on her pillow as her head fizzed with questions that needed urgent answers. How big would Egg grow? What sort of creature would he turn into? How could she keep him safe and secret? She knew that she wasn't going to be able to sleep until she had some answers, so, with Egg tucked under the flap of her dressing gown, Ginny crept quietly down the stairs and into the front room where the computer was.

The sudden brightness when she switched on the light in the room made both Ginny and Egg blink. She put Egg on to the floor, and he buried his face in the hem of the long curtain to shield his eyes from the light. Then he held the curtain between his paws and peeped one bright dark eye from behind it, and squealed, willing Ginny to join him in a game of peepo.

'I've got to work, Egg, so shush,' she told him. She switched on the computer.

Ginny looked up *dragons* and found that there were over two million entries on them. She found that dragons were *legendary creatures, typically with serpentine or reptilian traits, that feature in myths in many cultures.* She read that dragons *have scaly skin and are generally represented with wings, and sometimes breathing out fire.* Ginny chewed a finger. *Breathing out fire.* That made dragons sound like monsters.

'But they're wrong anyway,' said Ginny.
'Because you're not mythical, you're real, Egg.'
Ginny glanced behind her, expecting to see Egg
still by the curtain, but he'd gone. 'Egg?' Then
she saw him, swinging from the curtain high up.
He was chewing the curtain fabric to bits with
sharp little teeth. 'You bad boy!' she told him.
'Stop it!'

Egg skidded down the curtain, and began a new game with something behind the sofa, as Ginny turned back to the screen, searching for any information there might be about dragon babies. There didn't seem to be any to find. All she could see were pieces about the dragon that St George killed because it was eating girls, and . . .

BANG! Something exploded and the room went dark.

9

You Want Your Mum

'Egg? What have you done now?'

Ginny's eyes were adjusting
to the dim light from the street
lamp outside, and she could see
a small green nose poking round
the far side of the sofa. Two dark
eyes followed, and then all of the
rest of Egg became clear. Egg was
chewing the flex that ran between

the tall lamp stand and the wall.

As Ginny gasped in alarm, he ran clumsily over to her. He pulled the whole lamp over behind him, and the bulb exploded. Hundreds of sharp slithers of glass glinted on the wooden floor as he buried his nose in her dressing gown. Ginny reached down and picked him up.

'You might have been electrocuted,' said Ginny, hugging Egg tight, both of them shaking with shock. 'I bet you've woken Gran and Dad.' But nobody stirred upstairs.

So Ginny put Egg on to the sofa as she swept the broken glass into a dustpan and tried to tuck the curtain so that its frayed edge didn't show. And all the time she did that, she talked to soothe Egg, and to soothe herself. She felt tearful and wobbly and scared.

'There are nice things about dragons too, you know. The stupid computer just doesn't have them at the top of their things about dragons. What about dragonflies? They're beautiful and don't hurt anything. And snapdragon flowers that Gran grows. They're lovely too.'

Ginny crept back upstairs and put Egg and herself back to bed. But she couldn't sleep. She was half relieved, but half upset that neither Dad nor Gran had come running to find out what had made that sound. What Ginny really wanted was for Mum to give her a hug and make things right. Could she tell Mum about Egg in the hospital tomorrow?

Ginny looked at Egg, snoring beside her in the dim yellow street light that came through the curtains, and suddenly she did understand him.

'You want *your* mum, too, don't you? You want your *real* mum, not me.'

Ginny lay there, thinking about the dragon mother who must have laid the glistening egg that Egg had hatched from. Why would a dragon mother leave an egg in a henhouse? Might she be looking for her baby now, wanting him back? Would she be one of those huge, fierce dragons like the ones in the in computer pictures? Ginny looked at Egg.

'She'll think that I've stolen you!' Ginny glanced towards the window. Through the gap in the curtains, the night looked as blank as it usually did. There were no strange sounds that Ginny could hear. But she daren't get out of bed to look. There might be a dragon mother outside, waiting. Egg stirred, then gazed up at Ginny.

'Your mum will come and find you,' she said. 'I would if I was her. So we need to be ready for when she . . . Oh!' A thought suddenly came to Ginny. 'But she won't come *here*, will she? She'll go to the henhouse. That's it! So I'll put you back in the henhouse, Egg. Those hens know about looking after babies that come out of eggs. You'll be in the right place when your mum comes back. And I can visit Mum and the baby.'

Perfect. At last Ginny slept.

10

You're Going Home

Ginny was up and dressed before it was light.
Her body longed to stay in the warm bed, but she
knew that Egg must be moved now, before Dad
or Gran were up.

'Come on, Egg,' she told the sleepy dragon.
'You're going home.'

As she opened the back door and stepped
outside, the cold morning air turned Ginny's
breath into plumes of steam like dragon smoke.
Egg was a warm, wriggling bundle zipped into
her jacket and held firmly under her right elbow.

'You stay there,' she told him as he struggled
to get his head out to see where they were going.
'You've got to stay hidden in case we meet
anyone.' That was part of it, but it also helped

Ginny not to have to look into his trusting eyes, and know that she was about to leave him.

Ginny hardly recognised her own road as she walked up it towards Gran's house. The orange street lamps lit the front gardens and the cars parked along the road with a light that took away colour. The curtained windows down the street had a look of eyes, closed in sleep.

There were no sounds except the whine of a milk float in a neighbouring street and a distant swishing of wind in trees. Ginny could hear her own footsteps in a way that she had never noticed them before. If the great dragon mother was out looking for her, then her sound and movements would make her easy to spot. Ginny glanced all around, turned into Gran's garden, and ran down it towards the big hen run.

'It'll be nice having all those hens to mother you,' she told Egg. 'Your mum left you with hens because she knew they would look after you, didn't she? I'm sure she did.'

The hen run looked cold and bleak in the grey light with its bare earth and wire fencing – very different from the cosy bedroom Egg was used to.

'Still,' said Ginny, unzipping her jacket to

let Egg out, 'the hens will be nice and warm.
All those feathers! They probably talk the same
language as you. They'll understand you better
than I do.' Ginny looked down at Egg in the
gloom, and smiled encouragingly. When Egg
slow-blinked at her with trusting big eyes, she
nearly pushed him back into her jacket and ran
home.

They'd disturbed the sleeping hens, and now
they were scrabbling around in the henhouse,

wanting to be let out into the run and given their morning scattering of grain. Their clucking on the other side of the wooden walls didn't sound anything like that beautiful, lilting dragon song. Ginny wavered. She thought of the dragon mother, out there somewhere. Then she thought of her own mother and her baby brother. Ginny pulled open the henhouse door, and waded through the flurry of fussing hens.

'Here you are, Egg,' she said brightly. 'Back where you came from. Home.'

She put Egg down on the dusty, dirty floor, and busied herself with getting the hens' food and water. Would Egg share the hard yellow grain and musty pellets? In the shadowy, murky, morning light he looked small and strange, even though he was the same size as the hens now. His eyes were big and innocent when compared with the sharp little eyes of the hens. 'But you should be with flying creatures,' said Ginny. 'Ones that come out of eggs.'

He looked at her.

'You'll be happy here,' she said.

Still he looked.

Ginny turned and went, closing the gate

firmly between him and her. But his look tugged at her all the way back down Gran's garden, all the way down the road, and home. 'I should be feeling free,' she told herself, but the sick feeling of worry remained, and a new thought struck her. 'Gran will see him with the hens! Oh, I'll just have to tell her about him now.'

11

A Real Brother

There was no chance to talk to Gran alone that morning. As soon as breakfast was over, Ginny and Dad drove across town to the hospital.

The hospital was big and had a funny bathroom sort of smell to it. Dad knew his way along corridors and past lots of doors until they came to the maternity ward.

'Which room is Mum in?' asked Ginny, her stomach fluttering.

'She's over here,' said Dad, and he pointed to a closed door. Dad knocked on the door and waited.

'It's only Mum!' said Ginny. 'Why are you knocking?'

Mum was in a room all on her own. There were no other mothers, and, Ginny suddenly realised, no babies in there.

'Where is he?' she asked. Her hands went up to her cheeks as if she needed to hold her head steady while her mind spun with awful possibilities. 'Where *is* he, Mum?'

Mum was almost as white as the hospital sheets and walls, with big dark panda eyes in her pale face. The only bright thing in the room was the little pile of untouched patchwork fabrics on the bedside table.

'Ginny, love! Come here.' Mum's voice sounded a bit wobbly, but her arms went out. Ginny hugged Mum. She felt different without so much baby bump to cushion her front.

'Where's the baby, Mum?' Ginny asked again, more gently. 'The other mothers in the ward have all got their babies with them. Where's ours?'

Mum held Ginny and looked intently at her. 'Do you really want to see him? Has Dad told you . . .'

'About him having Down's syndrome? Yes. And *of course* I do!' Ginny stamped her foot as she said it.

'It's just . . .' Mum shook her head slightly. 'It's just that he looks different from other babies, you

see. He *looks* like a baby with Down's syndrome, and not, well, not like *my* baby, somehow.' Mum's mouth began to quiver, and Dad put his arm around her. Mum took a deep breath. 'He's in the nursery, Gin. One of the nurses is giving him a feed. Dad can take you along there if you want.'

Ginny took Dad's hand and dragged him through the door and across the corridor to the nursery. A nurse stood there, cuddling a bundle. The baby in the bundle had lots of spiky dark hair capping his pink face. The nurse looked up and smiled.

'You must be big sister,' she said.

Ginny stroked the silky, wet-looking hair on the baby's hot little head while the nurse wiped dribbles from his mouth and chin. The baby's eyes were closed slits lined by long dark lashes. Ginny longed to see them open. The nurse nodded her head towards a chair. 'Here. You sit down, love. See if you can get him to take a little more milk.'

Ginny settled herself firmly back into the chair and cradled her arms ready for the baby. He was heavy and solid feeling, but still very wobbly as the nurse tipped him gently into her arms. Gran had said that he was small for a newborn baby, but when Ginny thought that only hours before he had been inside Mum, he seemed huge!

Supporting the baby's neck and shoulders with her left arm, Ginny held the bottle in her other hand and touched the teat to his lips. The baby's pink mouth opened, and Ginny was surprised by the pull that sucked it in. She grinned up at the nurse, and the nurse smiled back. 'He wouldn't take any more from me,' she said. 'You're doing well.'

The baby drank the whole bottle of milk from Ginny. Ginny handed the bottle back to the nurse, and then had a good look at her brother. He had a squarish, fat-cheeked face of the most beautifully fine, soft, pale skin. He had slightly almond-shaped blue eyes that opened once his concentration on drinking had finished. He looked quizzically up at Ginny and the movement wrinkled his forehead.

'Hello,' Ginny whispered, and then she couldn't think of anything else to say.

He has a snub nose like mine, thought Ginny. And all that fine black hair. Ginny could see that in some ways the baby did look like Mark at school. But Mark had ginger hair and freckles. This baby felt and looked like a real brother to Ginny. She squeezed him in a gentle hug. So why didn't he feel like her own baby to Mum? 'Hello,' she said again. 'I'm your sister.'

The baby's eyes wandered in an unfocused way that didn't really look straight at her. Just like Egg's had when he was newly hatched, she thought. Ginny wondered how Egg was getting on with the hens. She gazed towards the window and then shook her head. She looked back into her brother's bright blue eyes. They're the colour of the sky on picture postcards, she thought. And his hair was the same deep black as Egg's eyes. 'One day soon you'll meet him,' she told her little brother.

'Who's he going to meet?' asked Dad, and Ginny looked up in surprise to see Mum, with

Dad, standing in the doorway and watching her.

'He's beautiful, Mum,' she said. 'But he does need a name. Everybody needs a name, and we can't just call him "the baby" all the time.'

That seemed to make Mum shrink back towards the door. 'Oh, not yet, Ginny. There's plenty of time to think about that later.' Mum pulled at her dressing gown, hugging it around herself, even though the hospital was hot. 'Come back to my room, Gin. Tell me all about home,' said Mum, and out she went.

'Can't the baby come with us?' said Ginny.

'Better not,' said Dad softly. 'Give him back to the nurse for now.'

At least Dad looked at the baby as he said it, thought Ginny. Mum didn't even do that. The nurse held out her arms to take the baby, and Ginny reluctantly handed him back. 'See you very soon,' she said, then she followed Dad to Mum's room.

When Ginny looked back from the doorway, she saw that the nurse had her baby brother propped over her shoulder and was jiggling him up and down and humming to him. The nurse laughed as the baby belched into her ear.

She seemed to be enjoying him. It should be Mum doing that, thought Ginny. And it should have been Mum feeding him too. Feeding him properly with breast milk, as she had seen Mum doing with her in photographs. There seems to be more wrong with Mum than with the baby, she thought.

12

Why?

In the car on the way home Ginny asked Dad why. Why wasn't Mum looking after the baby? Why hadn't he got a name yet? Why . . .

'Oh, Ginny, please give it a rest!' said Dad, but then he sighed. 'I'm sorry, love, but it's so hard to explain. You've just got to accept that having a disabled baby has been a shock, particularly for Mum. We've got a lot of thinking and adjusting to do before we're ready to – well – to decide how we are going to cope, I suppose.'

'He's disabled and we can't change that, so what is there to think about?' asked Ginny.

'Oh.' Dad swept a hand through his hair. His hair needs a wash, thought Ginny. 'Just stop the endless questions, please. It's nothing for you to worry about.'

A horrible thought suddenly came to her. In spite of what Dad had said, she couldn't not ask. 'You wouldn't give him away, would you, Dad? Have him adopted?'

'Ginny, please!' said Dad. 'Just stop it!'

Ginny laid her head against the back of the car seat. She remembered seeing on the television news once about disabled babies waiting for families to adopt them because their own families didn't want them. Was that what Mum and Dad had to have time to think about? Were they thinking about giving the baby away? Ginny felt so angry she wanted to shout something to shock Dad, to make him feel awful for not bringing the baby and Mum home, and making everything normal. But then she remembered Egg. She had handed him over to the hens. Was that any different?

Ginny's thoughts spun and she tried to reason with herself. It was for Egg's sake, she thought. 'It was to get him back to his mother.' But perhaps she was just making excuses? Perhaps she had been wrong to leave him with those scratchy hens? Ginny's hands were cold and clammy, and she felt a bit sick. She hadn't meant either to

steal or to dump Egg, and yet she had done both
of those things. She closed her eyes and tried to
think. As she sat in the car, with her eyes shut,
she felt a chilling, cold, dark shadow sweep over
her from outside. In her mind's eye she saw it
all: the dragon mother's vast wings blanking out
the sun as she plummeted down towards the car.
At any moment now there would be a ripping,
rasping noise of great dragon talons piercing
the car roof and working up and down, up and
down, like a tin opener opening a can of beans.
The dragon mother would peel back the roof
and pluck Ginny out of her seat. A sudden roar

came from outside the car window and Ginny felt heat on her face and saw fiery red through her eyelids. Dragon fire? She opened her eyes to grey, billowing smoke and screamed, 'No!' before something hit her hard on the head.

'What on earth are you playing at?' yelled Dad.

A car behind them honked.

'You nearly caused an accident!' Then Dad saw Ginny rubbing her head where it had bumped the back of the seat when he had suddenly braked because of her scream. 'Are you all right?' he asked more gently.

'Yes,' said Ginny.

She saw now what had really happened. A great noisy lorry was driving away from the traffic lights beside them. It must have shaded them from the sunshine as it came alongside and then revved its engines and belched out exhaust as it pulled away. 'You stupid thing!' she told herself silently. 'You imagined it all.'

Dragons didn't exist in real life, did they? Had she just imagined Egg as well? She urgently needed to find out.

'Dad, can you drop me off by Gran's and I'll walk the rest of the way home?'

'Yes, if that's what you want,' said Dad.

He'll be glad to be rid of me, thought Ginny.

Dad and Ginny drove the rest of the way to Gran's in silence, each of them deep in thought.

13

The Fire Monster

Ginny hurried down Gran's garden path. The
sun was shining now, the birds were singing and
everything should have felt fine . . . but it didn't.
Ginny looked anxiously towards the hen run to
see whether Egg was out with the chickens. She
was looking for green movement, but what caught
her eye was the lazy, menacing swirl of grey,
curling out from around the henhouse door.

Smoke.

Ginny ran.

'Egg!' she called. 'Oh, please, Egg!'

Ginny could see and hear the chickens
fussing and flapping out in the run, but Egg
wasn't with them. He must have still been in
the henhouse. In her mind Ginny saw the dry

straw bale, the wooden floor, doors and roof, and she knew that any fire in there would soon take hold.

Ginny couldn't see any flames through the dusty henhouse window but the smoke was thick, making her cough as it leaked between the plank walls. As she wrenched the door open, the smoke came at her thickly, grabbing at her throat and making her cough. For a moment it halted her in the doorway, but Ginny knew that Egg must be inside somewhere, and she had to go in. Ginny put her arms out in front of her and swam them through the smoke as she stepped inside and searched, eyes wide and streaming from the stinging smoke. At first she couldn't even see where the musty grey smoke was coming from. There was so much of it, smothering everything and choking her mind as much as her lungs. Ginny felt dizzy and sick and knew that she had to breathe some fresh air and think. Putting her head out through the doorway for a quick gulp of air, she pulled back from panicky thoughts.

'Come on! Think sensibly or you'll waste any chance to save him!'

Ginny put an arm up to muffle her mouth and nose from the smoke with her jumper sleeve. 'Where did you leave Egg this morning? Come on, think!' she bullied herself. Ginny closed her eyes and saw more clearly in her mind than her eyes could manage in the smoky hut. She saw Egg, small Egg, down in a corner on the floor.

Ginny crouched. The smoke was thinner lower down. Of course it was! Why hadn't she remembered? She knew perfectly well that smoke rises and gets thickest up at the ceiling. She remembered that in a fire you should stay low, get out of the building, and shut the doors behind you. And she was still in the hut with the door wide open! The air would soon stoke the smoky smouldering mess into real fire. It was happening already. Ginny saw one bright spark of orange flame blink on the floor in a corner. It wavered uncertainly for a moment, and then puffed into bold, scorching fire. Ginny instinctively put up her hands to shield her face, but just before they covered her eyes she glimpsed, in the new light from the fire, a small huddled dragon.

'Egg!'

Ginny plunged her hands through the flames,
down and up, bringing Egg out of the fire.
Clutching him to her, coughing and blinking
with streaming eyes, she stamped furiously at the
flames. They had tried to kill Egg, and now she
was going to kill them. But, as if it were playing
some sort of nightmare game, the fire seemed to

enjoy her stamping. Fire danced around her feet, leaping into new areas of straw and flaming them into the game too.

It can have the henhouse, thought Ginny. Just as long as Egg is safe! She knew she must get out of the hut before the whole thing exploded into flame.

'Get out!' she shouted.

Ginny stumbled out into daylight, gasping for air. The garden hose lay beside the henhouse. Ginny gently placed Egg down on a clump of grass away from the hut, and then ran her shaking legs up the garden to turn on the tap outside Gran's back door.

Grabbing the hose, Ginny aimed its shining silver blade of water into the orange heart of the fiery henhouse as it crackled and flickered and breathed out smoke. She stepped towards the burning heat, and felt as though she were going into battle with the terrible dragon mother that she had been dreading. Heat and fear prickled and stabbed at her, and she felt that the henhouse's flaming mouth might crash closed and chew her back into the fire. Clenching the hose tight between her hands, she swung the spear of water

across the flames, and the fire monster sizzled
with rage. At last it died to a few steamy breaths.
Coughing, shaking, but glad, Ginny stepped back
from the smoke into the cool, clear garden air,
and let the hose drop from her hands.

'There!' she said, and she pushed the hair and
smoke from her face. The blackened wisps of
straw blowing in the slight breeze looked pathetic.
Ginny felt a bit like Dorothy in *The Wizard Of Oz*
when she throws water at the Wicked Witch and
the witch sizzles and dissolves away.

Then Egg whimpered and, as surely as
the water had quenched the fire, worry about
Egg quenched Ginny's feelings of triumph.
She crouched down beside the soot-smeared,
shivering little dragon, put a finger under his
slumped head, and lifted his chin up.

'Egg?' she said.

Egg looked at her. His body was dulled with dirt
and pain but his eyes opened wide and glittered
as he slow-blinked a loving hello. He opened his
mouth and sang a ringing cry of welcome.

'You're glad to see me!' whispered Ginny,
amazed. 'Oh, Egg, why – when I left you here? It
was my fault!' She patted him clumsily as tears

poured down her face, washing the soot from her eyes. 'It'll be hard work,' she told the little green head that now rested and hummed happily against her chest. 'But I am going to keep you properly now, I promise. At home again.' And Ginny suddenly knew that she didn't dread the dragon mother any more. Perhaps she would never even come back for her child, and Egg could stay with her for ever.

'Come on, Egg,' she said, wiping grimy tears from her face and standing up. 'Let's go home.'

As she stood again, Ginny felt like a dirty jelly, grubby and wobbly, and she wasn't sure that she could hold on to Egg without dropping him. She sat down again and rested Egg on her lap while her ears and mind buzzed. Egg's scales were dull beneath the soot.

'My poor little Egg,' she said. There was a crusting of dark dried blood down the front of his neck and under his belly. 'On all your soft parts,' she said. 'Those hens! They've been pecking at you, haven't they? And I thought that they would look after you.' Ginny frowned. 'But who started the fire?'

Ginny thought about what the internet had

told her about dragons breathing fire.

'Was it you?' she asked the little face.

Egg gazed back.

Ginny closed her eyes. She could imagine it all. She opened her eyes and stroked Egg's head, over and over. 'You breathed out fire to frighten away the hens.'

Egg slow-blinked.

'And that set fire to the straw. Oh, Egg, you mustn't ever do that again! Not if I'm going to keep you! Now I really will have to talk to Gran about you.'

14

This Is My Dragon

Back home Ginny was glad to see Gran in the
kitchen getting lunch. She felt very strange,
pushing open the kitchen door and standing
there, dirty and smelling of fire and holding a
young dragon in her arms. Gran turned at the
sound of the door opening, and stood and stared.

'Gran, I . . .' Ginny faltered, not knowing
where to begin. But the sound of Ginny's voice
seemed to bring Gran to her senses, and Ginny
found herself guided from the doorstep and into
a chair.

'Whatever's happened, Gin? You look awful!'

As Gran filled the kettle for a hot drink, and
pulled muddy shoes off Ginny's feet, Ginny felt
something that had been cold and hard and strong

inside her begin to melt. When she spoke again her voice wobbled. 'There's been a fire, Gran. In your henhouse. I've put it out, but it's a mess.'

'Oh, my poor Ginny,' said Gran. 'I should have guessed.'

'Why?' said Ginny. 'How could you have guessed?'

Egg stirred in Ginny's arms, and snuffled a sooty sneeze. Ginny looked at Egg, settling on her lap for a rest, as large as a puppy now, and very obviously real. She looked up. Gran was watching Egg too, watching with a fond smile twitching at one end of her mouth.

'Gran!' exclaimed Ginny. 'Why don't you say something?'

Gran's mouth smiled at both ends now. She didn't look in the least surprised. Ginny tried again. 'Gran, this is my dragon. He's called Egg.'

'And he's a dear little fellow,' said Gran.

'He's a *dragon*, Gran. A real dragon!'

'Yes, I know, love. I've met one before.'

Gran smiled at Ginny's astonished expression.

'I had a little dragon of my own hatch out and stay when your grandad died,' she said. Gran looked away, and Ginny knew that she was looking back at memories. 'Do you know, I had forgotten all about her until I realised that you had found a dragon too.' Gran laughed. 'I remember being very cross with all the extra work she was!' Gran stroked the top of Egg's head and tickled behind his ears. 'I was worn out with nursing your grandad, and then he died and I just wanted to shut myself away in the home that he and I had shared. I wanted to treasure the memories that were all that was left of Owen. I didn't want to bother with anyone or anything else. And then I found that blessed egg! I didn't want it. But there it was, helpless, and nobody else to care for it. So I kept it warm, and watched it hatch, and out came a little dragon. Do you know, Ginny, there were moments when I almost put that baby dragon out on to the pavement in the hopes that somebody else would find her and look after her? She exhausted me.' Gran smiled. 'And yet I loved her dearly because she loved me. I cried when my little dragon went. I missed her then.'

Gran looked down at Egg.

'What was your dragon called, Gran?' asked Ginny.

'I never called her anything but Dragon, I'm afraid,' said Gran. 'You see, I had no intention of keeping her at first. I wasn't even sure if she was real, or if I was just an old woman going a bit loopy after your grandad's death. Anyway, I didn't name her, and by the time I came to love her and want her, Dragon seemed to be stuck with that as her name.'

Ginny thought back to that time after Grandad's death when Gran had shut herself away in her house and they had hardly seen her for days. Mum had told Ginny that Gran 'needed time to grieve'. And all that time Gran had been busy with a baby dragon!

'Why didn't you tell anyone?' asked Ginny.
'Why didn't you tell Mum about your dragon? Or
me?'

'Well,' said Gran, 'I decided that the dragon
was quite enough to cope with without worrying
about your poor mum thinking I was going dotty.
And just when I was beginning to feel strong
enough to share Dragon with the rest of you, well,
it was time for her to go.'

'Go? Go where?'

Gran put a hand on to Egg's back and fingered
his growing wings. The wing lines reached halfway
down Egg's body now, and Ginny could see
leathery folds hidden under them. 'Your Egg is
almost ready to go,' said Gran quietly.

'No,' said Ginny. 'He isn't going anywhere. He
needs me.'

'Not for much longer,' said Gran.

'But I need him,' said Ginny. 'Where will he
go?'

'He will go back to his mother once he can fly,'
said Gran.

'But why?' asked Ginny. 'Why do dragon
mothers leave their eggs if they want the babies
back in the end?'

Gran shrugged. 'I don't know all the answers, Gin. I only know that that is what happened to Dragon. She flew off into the beautiful autumn sunset with her mother.' Gran gazed out of the window. 'It was one of those orange, glowing evenings when the sun sits on the horizon looking exactly the great ball of fire that it is. Dragon's mother came to my garden and I knew that my job was over. It was a beautiful and sad time.' Gran paused. 'I thought that I would never forget it, and yet I had, you know, until you reminded me just now.'

Ginny saw that Gran's eyes were full of tears. When Gran crinkled her eyes into a smile to cheer Ginny up, the tears tipped over and down her face. Ginny put an arm around Gran's waist, and buried her face in Gran's comfortable, soft stomach. Then she asked, 'Gran, was the mother dragon fierce? Was she big?'

Gran laughed. 'Do you know, Gin, I really can't remember her size, but I'm sure that she can't have been frightening – I wouldn't have forgotten that.'

'How old was Dragon when she left you?'

Gran thought for a moment. 'I can't say how

many days old she was, but I do know that it was when she had learnt to fly. That was when she went.'

So there was some time left. Ginny wondered whether she could stop Egg from ever learning how to fly, and then he would stay with her for ever, wouldn't he? Gran clipped the wings of her hens to stop them from flying, but Ginny knew

that she couldn't do a thing like that to Egg.

'I'll go and clean Egg up,' she told Gran. 'He's dirty and he's been hurt.'

'And I'll go and see what sort of state that henhouse is in,' said Gran.

Up in the bathroom Ginny found some cotton wool, and filled a bowl with warm water. She sat on the closed toilet seat, put a towel across her lap and then put Egg on to the towel. As she carefully bathed the soot away, the damp scales down his back glowed their wonderful green-grey-blue-purple colours just as pebbles in rock pools show colours that are hidden when they are dry.

Ginny took fresh cotton wool and dabbed at the bloody wounds on Egg's neck and belly. His dark eyes flickered with pain as she touched him, but he stayed still and gazed at her. Ginny felt a bit as though she were a dragon too. She had tough armour that could keep her safe from some things, but she knew that she had a soft underbelly. She had been strong through the danger of the fire, and yet she hurt now.

'I'm sorry that I left you with those hens, Egg.'

She felt muddled. She knew now that Egg
would go back to his dragon mother. It was just
what she had hoped for only a few hours ago, so
why wasn't she happy about it?

Egg slow-blinked at her and she kissed the
top of his head.

That evening, Dad brought Mum home from the
hospital with him. Ginny hugged her so hard
that Mum could hardly breathe. Mum hugged
Ginny back just as hard.

But they came home without the baby.

'Where is he?' asked Ginny. 'Mum, what
have you done with him?'

Mum turned away from Ginny's intent face,
but Dad held Ginny by the shoulders and told
her, 'We haven't done anything with him, love.
He's at the hospital and will stay there for a
few days. The people at the hospital thought it
would be a good idea for us to leave him for a
day or two, just to give Mum and me some time
to sort things out. He's being well cared for.'

'But . . .' began Ginny, and this time Mum
spoke.

'Just be patient with us, please, Ginny. It

would really help if you would leave us to think about things in peace.' Then Mum turned her back on Ginny and went inside.

Ginny was stunned. Leave them in peace? Of course she wanted to help Mum and Dad, but not by leaving them and the baby alone!

15

Oh, Egg!

Mum and Dad stayed in the house. They said that they were resting and thinking, but it looked to Ginny as if they were just wasting time. Dad was using up his holiday from work and yet he wasn't doing the garden or decorating the bathroom walls that had been stripped of the old wallpaper months ago. He didn't practise his clarinet ready for the jazz concert. Mum didn't sew even one patch for the patchwork quilt. Worst of all, she and Dad didn't visit the baby.

'But we could go, couldn't we, Gran?' asked Ginny. She couldn't bear the thought of the baby all alone in the big hospital. What must he be thinking? She wanted to see and hold him again to reassure herself that her little brother was real even if Mum and Dad seemed to be pretending that he wasn't. But what about Egg? She couldn't take him with her to the hospital.

Ginny cradled Egg in one arm, stroking a growing wing with the other hand. She thought of how he had set fire to the hen house. 'You mustn't breath fire in this house, Egg! Just sleep, please, while I go and see my brother. You can have my cardigan,' she told him, and made a nest in a high-sided cardboard box. 'You'll be safe in there.' Egg had only breathed fire in the hen house because of the hens pecking at him, she thought. 'Sleep and don't worry,' she told him. 'I'll be back soon.'

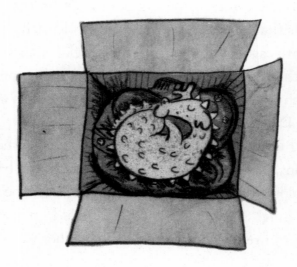

* * *

The hospital was bustling with visitors carrying bunches of flowers and teddy bears and other presents with pink or blue bows on them. Gran and Ginny hadn't brought anything. There didn't seem much point when the baby still had to wear hospital clothes and was too tiny and sleepy to be interested in toys.

'Here he is, Gran.' Ginny pointed to a clear plastic crib near the nursery's window. She was pleased that she could recognise him so easily. Some of the other babies looked very similar to each other but this one was her brother for sure. His black hair spiked up all around his head, and his blue, almond-shaped eyes were open.

'Hello, hedgehog!' whispered Ginny. She reached a hand into the crib and stroked the silky black hair down one side of his warm head. The baby's mouth opened and reached around towards her hand, his tongue working in and out.

Gran laughed. 'Oh, I remember what that means!' she said. 'He's hungry. I'll find a nurse and ask if he's due for a feed. Perhaps we will be allowed to give him his bottle.'

They spent about an hour with the baby. Ginny and Gran both tried feeding him. He drank some of the milk but kept spitting the bottle's teat out of his mouth. In the end they gave up trying to get any more into him, and Ginny held her little brother hugged to her shoulder as she had seen the nurse do on her last visit. He felt heavy to hold, and it made Ginny think about Egg again. Egg was still growing fast but he didn't seem to have got any heavier. Ginny had even begun to wonder whether he was actually getting lighter as he got bigger. The wonderful colours of his scales were certainly getting paler. Perhaps that was because they had to stretch to a bigger area as Egg grew, but Ginny felt that it was partly because Egg wasn't happy. It was strange. This baby, born on the day that Egg had hatched, was still all baby. His head flopped over and she had to support it with one hand. He felt warm and wriggly and smelt nicely milky. Ginny rocked from one foot to the other, and soon the baby slumped into sleep. Gran took him gently from Ginny and laid him back in the crib.

The baby lay curled with his knees up and

his legs down in a 'G' shape. His fists were up in front of his mouth. They had tiny white hospital mittens on them to stop him from scratching himself. Ginny thought that they made him look like a miniature boxer.

'We'll fight the world together,' Ginny promised him.

Back home, Ginny ran up the stairs.

'Egg!' she called quietly as she opened the bedroom door. 'I'm back.' She knelt beside the cardboard box on the floor.

But Egg wasn't there.

'Egg?' She looked under the bed. There was some fluff and a lost sock, but no Egg. 'Egg?'

Then she heard him, heard his singing chime from somewhere high up.

'Oh!' Ginny's hands went to her cheeks.

Egg was perched on the wardrobe, his tail curled, and a look on his face that showed that he thought he was being very clever.

'Oh, Egg, get down!' said Ginny. Then, as Egg wobbled on the edge of the wardrobe, she called, 'No, don't!'

Ginny stood with her arms held out ready

to catch him, but Egg didn't need catching. As
Ginny watched, he unfurled two wonderful wings
and gently flapped them to keep himself balanced
and the wings on show.

For a moment Ginny couldn't say anything.
She just watched. Egg suddenly launched himself
off the wardrobe and, flapping his wings rather
clumsily, he began to circle the room.

'Oh, they're beautiful!' said Ginny.

The wings shimmered pale grey-green-purple,
oil-in-a-puddle colours. They were delicate and
strong at the same time, and they reminded
Ginny of Gran's hands.

As he flew, Egg became more confident and

100

flapped less frantically. He glided and soared. As he swooped under the light that hung in the middle of the ceiling, the colours of his wings shone bright and clear.

Ginny sat down on her bed. She needed to get out of the way of the flying dragon, but she also suddenly felt too busy in her brain to cope with standing up. Egg swooped down to land on the bed beside her. He folded the wonderful wings and laid his head against Ginny's chest, humming gently into her body.

'It's time for you to go, isn't it?' said Ginny.

16

Kite

'What's the matter, Gin?' asked Mum the next morning. 'You look worried.'

Gran saved Ginny from having to answer. 'Maggie, why don't you and Stephen go out for a little walk this morning? It's a lovely sunny day and I'm sure that the fresh air would do you both good.'

With a smile and a wink at Ginny, Gran bundled Mum and Dad into boots and coats and almost pushed them out through the front door.

'Are you trying to get rid of us?' laughed Mum.

'Yes!' said Gran very firmly. 'Go and walk up Easter Hill, and don't come back until lunchtime.'

Once Mum and Dad were safely out of the

way, Gran turned to Ginny.

'Now then, chicken, you've got a job to do.'

Ginny pushed her tangled hair out of her
eyes and started to stack the breakfast bowls and
plates. 'My turn to wash up,' she said.

'No,' said Gran. 'I think you know what really
needs to be done.' She put an arm around Ginny,
and pointed up at the ceiling. 'That little one
needs his dragon mother now,' she said.

'Yes,' agreed Ginny. 'He's been flying.' Then,
'Gran, will you do it with me? Please?'

'No, love. You have to do this all by yourself.'

'Where should I take him?' asked Ginny.
'Where will his mother come to?'

'Back in my garden, where you found him,'
said Gran.

Ginny went upstairs, thinking about how
she must take Egg up the road to get to Gran's
garden, in daytime and with people about. Then
she would have to wait for the mother dragon.
And then she would have to say goodbye to Egg.

Egg was waiting on Ginny's bed, and he
slow-blinked when he saw her. She put her arm
around his soft tummy. He was so big now that
she couldn't reach all the way round him, but his

lightness made lifting him easy. Egg hummed into Ginny's chest while she thought about how she could carry him to Gran's garden. She couldn't hide him under her coat any more. He was just too big. Ginny stroked along the line of a folded wing.

'I know!' she said. 'You can fly!' Ginny imagined Egg rising up into the sky, and flying off the moment he saw his mother. That would be no good. She wanted to let him go when she was ready. 'I'll tie you on to a string, and you can pretend to be a kite,' she said.

Ginny found a long ball of wool and she tied one end around Egg's plump body. He snorted a giggle as she reached under his wings.

'Does it tickle?' she asked, and then, 'Does it hurt, Egg?' She was worried that the thin wool would cut into him. Perhaps something tucked under the string to pad it would help? 'Oh, I know!' she said, jumping off the bed and lifting the lid of her old dressing-up box. 'I'll turn you into a Chinese dragon with coloured streamers! If anybody stops me down the road, I'll just tell them that you're my Chinese New Year kite.'

Ginny took out three bright silk scarves

that Gran had given her ages ago for playing
magicians. She wrapped them around the wool
next to Egg's body. 'They'll look lovely when
you're flying,' she told him. 'And I bet they'll feel
nice too, streaming out behind you.'

Gran was at the door to say goodbye. She
patted Egg gently on the head. 'Send love to
Dragon for me if you see her,' she told him.
'Watch this, Gran,' said Ginny as she stepped

out of the doorway, and she threw Egg upwards towards the sky as she had seen racing-pigeon owners do with their birds. But Egg was no dull grey bird with clumsy, fluttering wings. Egg was magnificent. Ginny held on tight to the ball of wool as Egg soared with slow easy beats of his beautiful big wings. The bright sunshine glowed on them and lit up their array of colours, but it glowed through them too, so that Ginny could see the shapes of the clouds moving in the sky beyond.

'Isn't he wonderful?' she said, but Gran didn't reply. She just nodded and waved, her mouth tight closed. Ginny looked back and saw the sunlight glinting on Gran's brooch, and on her shiny eyes, before the door closed.

17

Eggstraordinary

Ginny walked up the road, letting the wool
unravel in her hands as Egg gained height.

'Don't pull,' she called to him.

He could easily tug the wool from her hand
if he wanted to. He was big enough and strong
enough. He could burn through the wool with
one hot blast of breath if he wanted to. But
he didn't. He rose gently and steadily, circling
upwards in the buffeting wind. His scales glinted
and sparkled like pale sequins, and Ginny
watched with a mixture of pride and sadness
lumping in her throat.

The only person that they met close up in the
short distance between the two homes was the
milkman. He took Ginny by surprise because he

stopped his milk float outside Gran's house.

'Hello,' he said. 'Your gran asked me to leave milk again today. She said she'd be going home.' And then the milkman noticed Egg. 'What's that, then? Some sort of remote-controlled toy?'

Ginny looked up. Egg, bored with waiting while the milkman chatted, was doing loop the loops at the end of his wool lead. Ginny wondered what she could say that would make the milkman lose interest.

'It's a Chinese New Year kite,' she began, but the milkman wasn't listening. He had one hand shading his eyes and his mouth was open in wonder.

'That's extraordinary!' he said. 'I've never seen anything that looks so exactly as if it was really alive!'

Ginny froze. Had he said *Egg*straordinary? Had he said *Egg*sactly? Did he know?

'Would you believe it?' said the milkman, 'I'd swear that was a real dragon on the end of that string.' He began to lift up his mobile phone to photograph Egg, and Ginny unfroze fast. She pulled the woollen thread to bring Egg around to have the sun directly behind him. The milkman

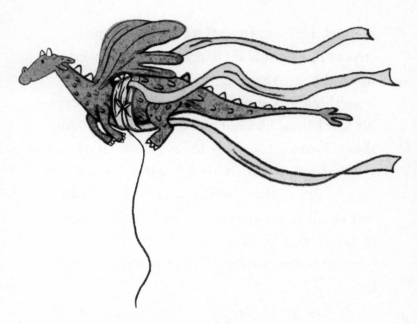

scrunched his eyes but still had to look away
from the dazzling brightness. And at the same
moment, Ginny kicked over the carton of milk
that the milkman had put on Gran's doorstep,
and, as the milkman bent to pick it up, Ginny
slipped through the side gate into the garden.

Safe.

The garden was strangely quiet. The hens
were cowering in the sooty henhouse as if they
were afraid of some unseen threat. It made
Ginny nervous. They can feel the mother dragon
coming, she thought. The air in Gran's garden

seemed different from the gusty wind in the street. The light had changed. Ginny looked up, and knew that Egg, too, could feel that something was about to happen. He had stopped his aerobatics, and hung in the air above Ginny, slowly beating his wings to keep himself airborne.

'Egg, come here.' Ginny began to pull in the long length of the woollen thread. Now that it was about to happen, Ginny was suddenly afraid of the mother dragon in a way that she hadn't been since the fire. She felt a strong instinct to hide.

As Egg gently flapped down, Ginny bundled the wool into her pouch pocket, and took Egg into her arms. She looked around the garden, searching for a place where they could hide.

It was too far to go to the house, and the climbing trees were still bare of leaves. They would have to hide in the henhouse with the hens. There was fresh, clean straw inside the henhouse, but the smell of fire was still strong as Ginny opened the door. She hesitated for a moment. It seemed odd to shelter in a place where she had fought a battle so recently, but the henhouse didn't feel threatening now. As Egg eagerly

watched the sky through the doorway, Ginny
knew that he would soon be gone. Then she
would be alone. She quite welcomed the company
of the silly hens.

'Chicken yourself!' she whispered.

Down on her knees in the prickly straw,
Ginny undid Egg from the tangle of silk scarves.
She put a protective arm around him and wished
that she could think of the right things to say to
him in what, she felt sure, were their last minutes
together. Egg seemed content as he leant against
Ginny, and she stroked down his neck and chest
and tried not to think of how much she was going
to miss him. The colours of his scales seemed
brighter now. Even in the dim light coming
through the soot-darkened window, his scales
glowed their colours. Ginny picked Egg up and
held him gently to her. He was so light that she
felt if she let go now he would just float up and
away.

'You're ready, aren't you?' she whispered, and
felt tears threatening. Crying would spoil things.
She must think about something else.

Ginny looked around her at the blackened
henhouse. Six pairs of beady yellow eyes watched

her as she clung to Egg. She picked up a burnt stick and wrote *Ginny luvs Egg* on the henhouse wall. But the writing would fade. She wished that she could think of something better, something beautiful to mark her love for the little dragon. She pushed the henhouse door open a little so that she could see more of the garden, hoping it would give her an idea.

As she looked into the garden, the stick dropped from Ginny's hand. 'Egg,' she whispered, 'your mum's almost here!'

18

They Belong

Gran's garden had changed since Ginny and
Egg had arrived. The light was different now.
Over towards Easter Hill the sky was dark and
wept heavy rain, but in Gran's garden it was
brilliantly, almost glaringly, sunny. Between the
two weathers a huge double rainbow arched like a
grand entrance to somewhere. The wind had gone
completely. Everything was still, still and waiting.

'Listen!' Ginny whispered.

Egg put his head on one side and, as he
listened, he quivered with excitement. A distant
beating noise was getting steadily louder. Wings,
big wings, thought Ginny. She rested her cheek
on the top of Egg's head.

'This is it, Egg.'

They watched through the henhouse doorway as a dark dot in the sky got steadily bigger. Soon Ginny could see the wings on either side of the dot, and she began to feel the air buffeting them as the dragon got nearer. Impatiently, she pushed her blown hair away from her eyes, determined not to miss any of this experience. The flapping of the large spoked wings startled Ginny with a memory of how Grandad, before he got ill, used to flap his big black umbrella in the doorway when he came in out of the rain. As the mother dragon flew out of the dull, rainy sky and into the bright sunlight of Gran's garden, Ginny could see her properly at last. She was no monster.

'She's beautiful, Egg!' Ginny whispered. 'She's like you.'

The mother dragon was dark bottle-green, with scales sparkling purple-blue, grey-green. She was iridescent like a magpie feather, but more so, magically more so. She was big but, like Egg, somehow insubstantial.

'She's lovely,' Ginny whispered. 'She's got kind eyes like Gran's.'

Ginny felt no fear at all now.

The mother dragon stopped beating her wings.

She held them steady, gliding in the air, and the commotion around Ginny stilled. The dragon came silently down on to the grass, and lifted up her head. She looked at Ginny standing in the doorway of the henhouse, and Ginny had the feeling that the dragon could see all her thoughts and secrets with her deep dark eyes. Ginny looked back. But there was something in those eyes that surprised Ginny. The mother dragon was unsure that Ginny would give her baby back, unsure that Egg would even want to go back to her! Ginny couldn't bear that hurt. She loosened her hold of Egg.

'He'll come to you,' she called softly to the mother dragon. 'I won't stop him.'

Still the mother dragon didn't move.

'Go on, Egg. It's all right. Go to your mum.'

Egg struggled, and Ginny realised that he was still tied to the woollen thread. She pulled a piece of the wool between her two hands. It cut into her hands but didn't break, so she put it between her teeth and bit through it.

Now Egg scrabbled clumsily through the doorway. He flap-ran straight to his dragon mother who lifted a vast webbed wing to bring him to her.

As they met, both dragons sang – Egg his ringing high-up chime, and the mother dragon a deeper, more resonant changing chord, but the sounds came together beautifully. Ginny shivered slightly now that the warmth of Egg had gone from her. She nursed the hand cut by the wool, and she watched as the two dragons, big and little, touched noses. Egg's colours glowed brighter than Ginny had ever seen them before. He squeaked one of his high up-and-down questioning squeaks and put his head on one side. The mother dragon sang deeply and steadily like a cathedral organ, and smiled down at him. They belonged together. Ginny felt left out now, but she could see that Egg was happy.

When the mother dragon looked towards Ginny again her eyes seemed to invite Ginny to come closer and be part of the dragon family for one last time.

'Yes,' said Ginny softly, 'I will.' She walked out of the cold, dark henhouse. The mother dragon lifted her wing again, and Ginny stepped under it and let its warmth and shelter canopy over both her and Egg. Sounds and sights from outside were all muffled by the wing, and for a few moments it felt as though she and Egg were the only creatures in the world. Egg came up to the height of Ginny's knees now, and she crouched down as he looked up at her with his dark eyes, and hummed happiness into her chest. 'Goodbye, Egg,' she said. That was all.

Then she let go.

A double chording chime of high and low dragon voices called a message back to Ginny, and quite suddenly the safe darkness lifted and a cold wind punched at her as the two dragons lifted up into the sky. Ginny shaded her eyes to watch as the mother and child rose up, circled overhead

and saluted her with dipped wings before speeding off fast towards the sun.

Ginny watched them get smaller and seem to melt together as the sunlight made her eyes water.

'Oh, come back!' called Ginny, but not loudly.

Ginny rubbed her eyes and looked again, but her eyes were filled with tears now and she couldn't see anything moving in the sky except some smudged white pigeons flying over the garden. She couldn't hear anything except the hens fussing their way back out into their run.

As Ginny stood and watched, cloud blotted out the sunlight, and it began to rain. Her arms felt strangely empty, but there was something smooth and warm that she unthinkingly turned over and over between her fingers. She folded her fingers around the object. Then, with rain and tears streaming down her face, she ran home. Egg had his mum now, and Ginny very much wanted hers.

19

Owen Stephen Abbot

As Ginny neared home she could see through
the window that Mum was with Gran in the
kitchen. She paused for a moment, half-hidden by
a tree, and felt the wetness on her face and knew
that there were sooty smudges on her jacket. If
it had just been Gran in the kitchen then Ginny
would have gone to her, but she couldn't go to
Mum in this state without all sorts of complicated
explanations. She wished that she could.

So Ginny crept around the house to the back
door. She dropped her dirty jacket by the washing
machine, and then went up to her room. She
closed her bedroom door, shutting out the sound
of happy chatter that came from the kitchen. She
went to the window and looked out and up the

road towards Gran's garden and the big sky beyond.
It was full of rain clouds now. There was no sun to
show which direction the dragons had gone. And
no dragons. No Egg. Ginny clenched her fists tight.

'Ow!' She cried out in surprise and pain as she
felt a sharp edge inside her fist, against the soft
part of her hand. She had forgotten that she was
holding something. Ginny uncurled her fingers and
looked down at a slim, silky-smooth, shiny shape
that glinted. It was a dark bottle-green colour, but
had rainbow colours hidden in the green that came
and went as she tilted it to and fro in the light.

It was like Gran's mother-of-pearl brooch stone,
only darker, thought Ginny, and then she laughed.
'Mother-of-Egg!' It must be one of the scales from
Egg's mother. 'Now I *have* got something to keep
for ever, something to remind me of Egg.' Ginny

wondered whether this scale was like Egg's, and would show its colours more brightly when it was wet. She decided to try it in the bathroom.

As Ginny opened her bedroom door she heard a small noise that wasn't chatter from Gran and Mum. It wasn't even from downstairs, she realised. She stood still to listen, and heard again a high-up little voice that sounded like it was saying, 'Lair'.

Hardly believing what she was thinking, Ginny stepped into the little bedroom next to hers.

'Oh,' she said, disappointed. The baby's cot was still empty. But . . .

'Lair!' said a little voice by Ginny's feet. She looked down to see her baby brother, eyes wide open, snugly nestled in a baby car seat on the floor.

'Hello, hedgehog!' Ginny whispered. She crouched down beside him and kissed his tickly, soft, spiky hair. A fat baby fist bumped her nose, and she offered him a finger. The baby clenched it hard. In her other hand Ginny still had her mother-of-Egg scale. She held it up and tilted it to and fro to catch the light and glint for the baby. The baby's hazy eyes watched, and his legs wiggled happily under their blanket wrapping. 'I'll tell you all about Egg one day,' Ginny told him. 'Perhaps he will come back and you will meet him.'

There was the sound of the front door opening, and then Dad's voice, 'Who's for fish and chips? Is our Ginny back yet, or should I put this lot in the oven to keep warm?'

'I noticed her jacket by the back door,' Gran was saying. 'I think that you may find her if you go upstairs, Maggie. Stephen and I will put things out on the table.'

Then there was the sound of Mum's footsteps hurrying up the stairs.

'Ginny?'

Ginny peeped round the door.

'Ginny!' Mum's smile looked as if it might swallow her ears, and she was laughing. 'Well, what do you think?' she asked as she put an arm round Ginny's shoulders and they looked together at the baby.

'Is he home for good?' asked Ginny.

'For good and for ever,' said Mum firmly. 'And he's not just "the baby" any more. He is Owen Stephen Abbot. Do you like it?'

'Owen like Grandad,' said Ginny. 'Yes.'

For a little while Ginny and Mum just looked down and smiled, and then Ginny said, 'He looks different. Do you think that's because he's got a name?'

'Perhaps that's part of it,' said Mum. 'But it's also the stripy babygro instead of the white hospital T-shirt and blanket.'

Mum knelt down and rocked the baby seat. She looked up and told Ginny about how she and Dad had walked up Easter Hill and decided that it was time to bring the baby home.

'I cried,' she told Ginny. 'I cried for the first time since Owen was born. I think that the wind and rain blew and washed away something during that walk. That and the talking. Anyway, we decided that we wanted our baby home, and we wanted to do it straight away. We didn't think to go home first for baby clothes or a car seat, but the nurses lent us this funny egg-shaped seat and Gran had left a bag of baby clothes in the hospital in case we might need them. My mum has always known me better than I know myself!' Mum smiled.

Ginny had to think for a moment before she realised that Mum was talking about Gran.

'Owen fell asleep in the car on the way home so we left him sleeping in his seat rather than disturb him by putting him in his cot. So yours was the first face that he saw at home.'

Ginny looked at Owen. He was asleep again, his mouth open, gently snoring.

'Come on,' said Mum. 'Let's eat that fish and chips before he wakes up. I'm hungry.'

20

Great Treasure

That afternoon, when Owen was asleep in his cot and Dad was digging the garden, Mum sat down with Ginny.

'Here, have a look at what I've been doing to our patchwork,' she said. She stretched out the bright patchwork of coloured memories and pointed to a new patch. It was a patch that wasn't colourful.

'Oh,' said Ginny, and then 'Oh!' again as she recognised the whitish material with a bit of black writing on one corner. 'The hospital baby T-shirt! A patch for Owen! Oh, good.'

'It's a bit dull,' said Mum. 'But it's special.' She smiled. 'The nurse let me take it.' And then the smile went, and Mum looked intently at Ginny.

'Sometimes it's the dull things, the ordinary things, that are the most important ones in life, Gin. That patch will always be particularly special to me.'

'And me,' said Ginny. She looked at Mum's serious face. 'Mum, can I tell you something?' Was it a good idea to tell? She did want Mum to know everything.

Mum nodded, so Ginny told her all about Egg. By the end of the telling, Ginny had tears running down her face and Mum's arms hugged around her.

'Egg sounds very special,' said Mum. 'I'm glad that he was here for you when I wasn't. It was a strange time for me too, Gin. When Owen was born with Down's syndrome I didn't know what to think or do. I just wanted to huddle into a safe shell away from everything. And now, well, I suppose I've hatched out into a world that is different from the one I was used to, but still one that I can be happy in. Very happy.' She gave Ginny a squeeze. 'Can you understand any of that?'

Ginny nodded.

'Good,' said Mum, sitting up properly and

reaching for the sewing box. 'Then let's finish off
this patchwork and turn it into a quilt to keep our
little Owen warm and snug.'

'OK,' said Ginny. 'You know, Egg was bright
colours like the quilt when he was happy.'

Mum raised her eyebrows. 'He must have
been very beautiful. Could you draw Egg for me?'

So Ginny got out pens and paper and drew a
little dragon with a green snub nose and multi-
coloured scales running from its head, down
its back and along its tail. She drew wonderful
webbed wings and a soft green underbelly.
Then she drew two deep dark eyes that seemed
to look right into you. She showed the picture
to Mum.

'Do you know,' said Mum, 'he reminds me of something . . .' She ran a finger down the little picture dragon's back. 'He's almost familiar. I wonder where I could have seen him before?' Mum shook her head and went back to threading her needle. 'Perhaps it'll come back to me,' she said.

'I hope that he comes back to me,' said Ginny.

When Owen woke up, Mum lifted him gently out of his cot. 'Hello, my treasure,' she said.

Treasure, thought Ginny, that's what dragons guard, isn't it?

Gran saw Ginny frowning. 'You're looking broody again, Gin. What is it this time?'

Ginny just shook her head slightly and smiled.

'Well,' said Gran. 'It seems that everyone is back where they should be except for me. I think that it's time that I went back home to my silly hens.'

'But will you help us do 'Bottoms' first?' said Ginny. 'We need you to hold Owen.'

Dad laughed. 'You don't really want to do that old thing, do you, Gin?'

But Mum replied for her. 'Yes,' she said firmly,

'we do.' She handed Owen to Gran, and they did 'Bottoms'.

'Mummy A-bot, Daddy B-bot,Ginny C-bot and Owen D-bot,' sang Mum. 'We've got one *more*, so now we are *four* . . . Bottoms!'

And Gran twiddled baby Owen around to bump his tiny nappied bottom and be hugged into the family circle. Ginny hugged Mum, Dad and Owen hard, and closed her eyes for a moment. And Egg is E-bot, she thought. I mustn't ever forget him.

About the Author

PIPPA GOODHART trained as a teacher before becoming a children's bookseller for ten years and is now a full-time author with over a hundred books published including award-winning *You Choose*, which has sold over a million copies. She also writes the *Winnie the Witch* storybooks under the pen name of Laura Owen.

Pippa lives in Cambridge with her husband and children.

Visit her website www.pippagoodhart.co.uk

About the Illustrator

ADRIA MESERVE grew up in New England, USA before moving to the UK at the age of twelve. She is a graduate of the Courtauld Institute of Art and studied for an MA in illustration at Brighton University. Adria has written and illustrated many picture books. Her most recent – *The Comedy, History & Tragedy of William Shakespeare* – is a colourful celebration of the world of Elizabethan theatre, and was commended at the SLA Information Book Awards. As well as writing and illustrating picture books she teaches art at a college in North London.

A DOG
CALLED FLOW

'I want a dog. I really want a dog.'

Oliver is finding it hard at school and he longs for
a dog. A dog could be a friend who doesn't care
whether or not he's good at school work.
When Oliver's parents say no to a dog,
Oliver gets his puppy in secret.
Will he be allowed to keep Flow?
Boy and dog are both tested at the local show,
and then face a challenge on the fells
that shows just what they're made of.

*'Powerful message about bravery, friendship
and the challenges of dyslexia,
delivered in a pacy, action-packed story.'*
Alexandra Strick of Inclusive Minds

'A book about real friendship and loyalty.'
Aaron, aged 10

Discover more stories

you'll love

at

troikabooks.com

troika